Curious George

BAKES A CAKE

Adapted from the Curious George film series
Edited by Margret Rey and Alan J. Shalleck

1 9 9 0

Houghton Mifflin Company, Boston

Library of Congress Cataloging-in-Publication Data

Curious George bakes a cake/edited by Margret Rey and
  Alan J. Shalleck.
    p.   cm.
  "Adapted from the Curious George film series."
  Summary: George gets in and out of trouble when he helps a friend
bake a cake.
  ISBN 0-395-55725-9
  [1. Monkeys—Fiction. 2. Humorous stories.] I. Rey, Margret.
II. Shalleck, Alan J. III. Curious George bakes a cake (Motion picture)
PZ7.C921363   1990   90-34015
[E]—dc20   CIP
                          AC

Printed in the United States of America

RNF ISBN 0-395-55725-9
PAP ISBN 0-395-55716-X

WOZ 10 9 8 7 6 5 4 3 2 1

"George," said his friend, "Jimmy's mom is
baking cakes today. How would
you like to go over and help her out?"

It sounded like fun to George,
so he went over to Jimmy's house.

"You're just in time to help me,"
said Jimmy's mom. "One cake's in the
oven and now I'm starting another one."

On the counter was everything Jimmy's mom
needed for making the cakes.

Next to a big bowl was a strange-looking
gadget. What was that for?
George was curious.

Suddenly Jimmy's mom stopped working.
"My necklace," she cried. "I know I put it on
this morning, and now it's gone!"

"George, please help me look for it."

George looked all over the kitchen.

"It's not here," said Jimmy's mom.
"I'm going to look upstairs."

Now George was alone.
What was in that bowl?

George jumped up and looked in.
Then he tasted the batter.
It needed something more.

He added eggs . . .

. . . some milk and all the flour.

He added some chocolate bits
but ended up eating most of them.

Now, what about that strange-looking gadget?

He pushed the red button.
The bowl started to go around –
faster and faster.

Batter flew out of the bowl, all over George,
the counter, the walls, and the floor.
What a mess!

When Jimmy's mom came back she was angry.
"What have you done, George?
Help me clean up this mess."

George picked up a broom and started to work.

Finally the kitchen was clean and it was
time to take the other cake out of the oven.

Jimmy's mom left the cake to cool. "I'm going
back upstairs to look for my necklace.
Stay out of trouble," she told George.

Mmmm. That cake smelled good.

George took a little piece.
Then a bigger one . . . and then one more.

Before he knew it, half the cake was gone.
But what was that?
He saw something shiny.

It was the missing necklace.
He pulled it out, put it on,
and then had some more cake.

Soon Jimmy's mom returned.
"George!" she cried.
"What happened to my cake?"

But when she saw that George had found
her necklace she gave him a big hug.

Just then George's friend came in.
"Anything left for me?"

Jimmy's mom gave him some cake and told him
how George had found her missing necklace.

"Good job, George," said his friend.
"You've been a real help."